WHAT WE LIKE

written and illustrated by ANNE ROCKWELL

Macmillan Publishing Company New York
Maxwell Macmillan Canada Toronto
Maxwell Macmillan International New York Oxford Singapore Sydney

for Nicholas and Julianna

Macmillan Publishing Company is part of the Maxwell Communication Group of Companies.

Macmillan Publishing Company
866 Third Avenue
New York, NY 10022

Maxwell Macmillan Canada, Inc.
1200 Eglinton Avenue East
Suite 200
Don Mills, Ontario M3C 3N1

First edition

Printed in the United States of America

10   9   8   7   6   5   4   3   2   1

The text of this book is set in 22 point Quorum Bold.

The illustrations are rendered in pen and ink and watercolor on paper.

Library of Congress Cataloging-in-Publication Data

Rockwell, Anne F.
    What we like / written and illustrated by Anne Rockwell. — 1st ed.
        p.   cm.
    Summary: Introduces words and concepts arranged in such categories as "What We Like to Make," "What We Like to Wear," and "What We Like to Eat."
    ISBN 0-02-777274-8
    1. Vocabulary—Juvenile literature.   [1. Vocabulary.]   I. Title.
PE1449.R64   1992   428.1—dc20   91-4990

Turn the pages of this book
and you will see

 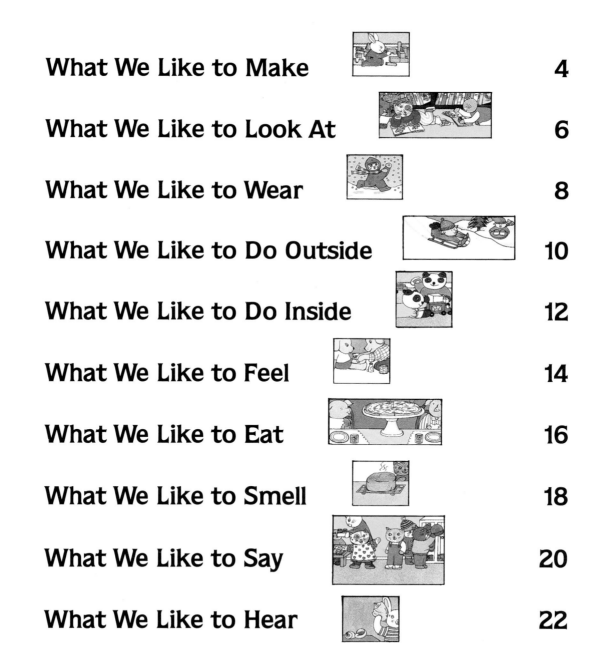

4 ◆ What We Like to Make

cookies

sand castles

paintings

clay statues

secret hiding places

bird houses

a snowman

cities of blocks

mud pies

macaroni necklaces

6 ◇ What We Like to Look At

picture books

tropical
fish

a face in
the mirror

little plants growing

a cozy fire

clouds in the sky

wrapped presents

the full moon

8 ◇ What We Like to Wear

warm pajamas

grown-up clothes

tights and tutus

Halloween costumes

new shoes

snowsuits

sunglasses

hats   hats   hats

bathing suits

rain gear

10 ◇ What We Like to Do Outside

go sledding

make noise

jump
in
puddles

ice skate

plant gardens

swing

jump in
autumn leaves

climb trees

drink from the hose

12 ◆ What We Like to Do Inside

play
hide-and-seek

play the piano

draw pictures

play
with dolls

listen to stories

count the stars

play with toy trucks

take bubble baths

grass under
bare feet

wiggly
worms

big hugs

smooth pebbles

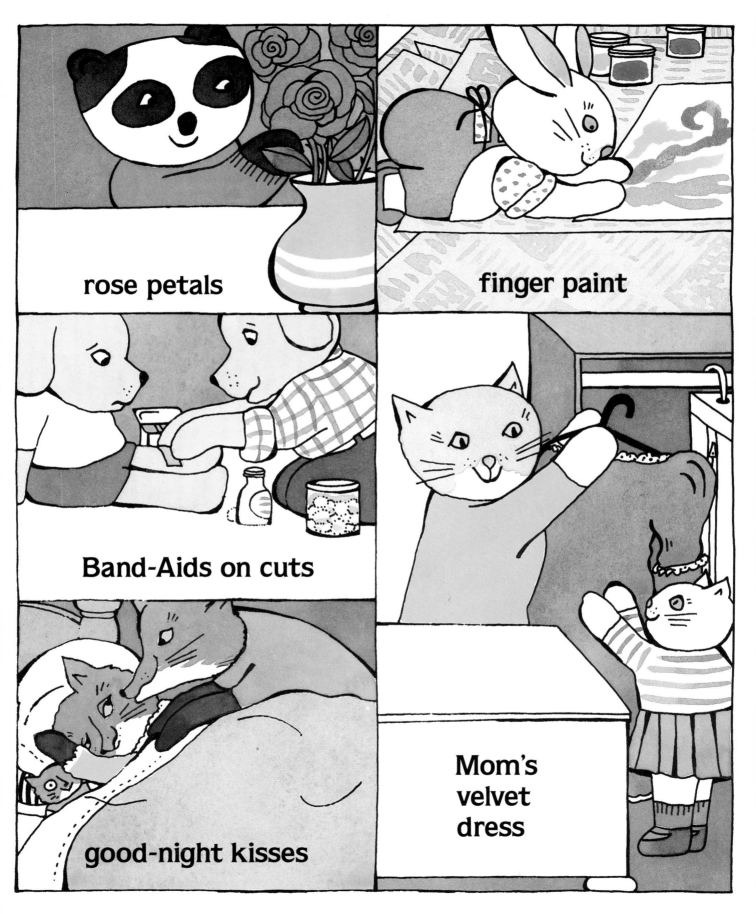

rose petals

finger paint

Band-Aids on cuts

good-night kisses

Mom's velvet dress

16 ◆ What We Like to Eat

pizza

berries

ice-cream cones

Easter eggs

peanut butter
sandwiches

 **17**

corn on
the cob

milk and cookies

the pudding
stirring spoon

popcorn

18 ◆ What We Like to Smell

daffodils

apples

bubble gum

new-mown grass

Christmas trees

fresh-baked bread

Mom's perfume

brand-new books

autumn leaves

Hi! My name is Julianna. What's yours?

Good morning

I know a secret

Thank you

I love you!

Can you come
over and play?

Catch!

the
ocean
in
a
seashell

my father's
harmonica

tick-tock!

birds singing

"let's share it"

rain on
the roof

grandmother's voice
on the telephone

lullabies

Now you tell me
what you like best.

Four Winds Press
Macmillan Publishing Company
866 Third Avenue, New York, NY 10022
First published 1988 in Great Britain by Walker Books Ltd, London
First American Edition 1989
Printed and bound in Italy
10 9 8 7 6 5 4 3 2 1
Library of Congress Cataloging-in-Publication Data
Roffey, Maureen.
Bathtime/Maureen Roffey.—1st American ed.   p.   cm.
Summary: Two youngsters who have gotten dirty playing prepare for
their bath, enjoy the adventure of getting clean again, and finish their
other preparations for bedtime.
ISBN 0-02-777161-X
[1. Baths—Fiction.] I. Title.
PZ7.R6255Bat 1988   [E]—dc19   88-21372 CIP AC

Bathtime

Maureen Roffey

FOUR WINDS PRESS
New York

There are so many ways
to get in a mess!

How do you get in a mess?

It's bathtime.
The faucets are on.

Water splashes. Water is wet.
What else can you say about water?

Time to get into the bathtub.

Which clothes do you take off first?

Which clothes do you take off last?

Bathtime is good for playing. Which
toys do you play with at bathtime?

Lots of things belong to bathtime.
How many of these do you have?

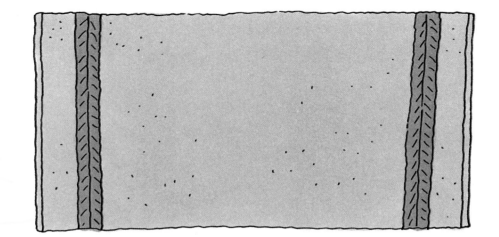

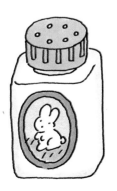

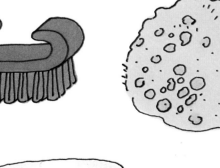

Baths are for washing all over.

Which parts do you wash at bathtime?

Bathtime is over. Pull the plug.

Where does all the water go?

Rub-a-dub-dub. It's drying time.

You dry your face . . . your arms . . .

your legs . . . your back.

What else do you dry?

What clothes do you put on after bathtime?

Don't forget your teeth...

and hair.

Now pop into bed.

Story time.
What is your favorite story?

Snuggle down.

Good night. Sleep tight.